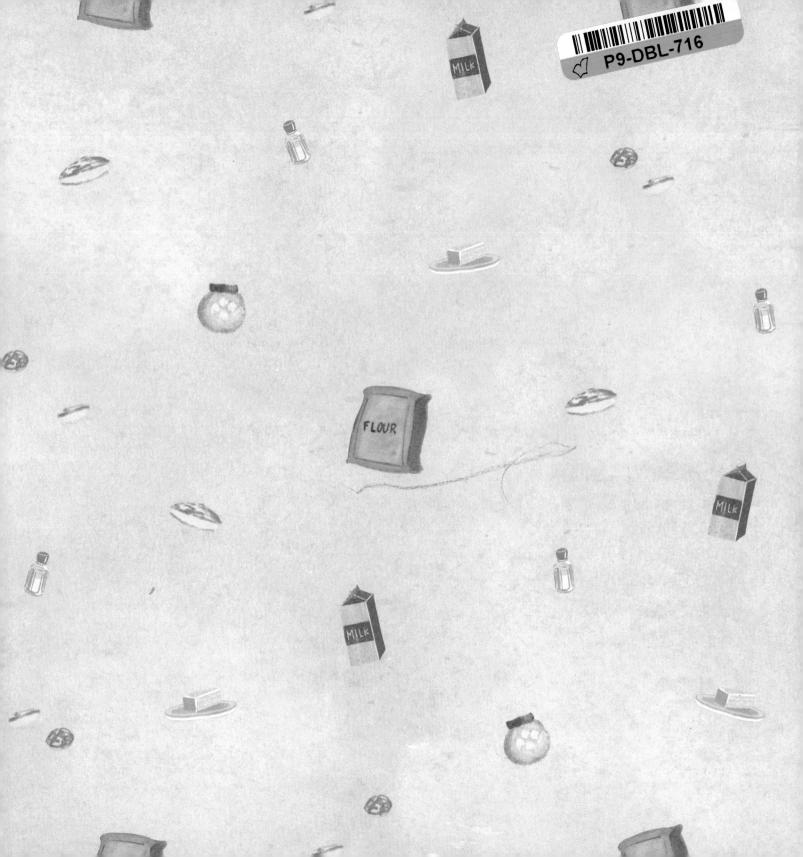

Awâsis

and the World-Famous

Bannock

Dallas Hunt

Amanda Strong

HIGHWATER
PRESS

For nôhkom, Helen McRee

—D.H.

For Olivine Bouquet

—A.S.

Awâsis spends every Sunday with Kôhkum.
One Sunday, Kôhkum asked Awâsis to take some
of her world-famous bannock to a relative.

Along the way, Awâsis jumped over rocks.

She ran through fields and skipped over bridges.

But then, while she was having so much fun, Awâsis dropped Kôhkum's world-famous bannock off a bridge.

Awâsis saw that she had lost Kôhkum's world-famous bannock. She started to cry.

Just then, Sîsîp waddled by and noticed Awâsis crying. "Tân'si nitôtem," Sîsîp quacked, "What's the matter?"

Awâsis replied, "I lost nôhkom's world-famous bannock. What do I do?"

"Don't worry," Sîsîp quacked. "I don't have any bannock, but I do have some tohtosapopimehkan, and I'm pretty sure that's in bannock!"

Awâsis smiled and gratefully accepted Sîsîp's offering. Awâsis continued on her way.

Just then, she saw Wâpos hopping to and fro.
"Tân'si nitôtem," Awâsis said, "Do you know
where I can find some bannock?"

Wâpos stopped hopping and replied, "Namoya,
Awâsis, but I have some askipahkwesikan,
and I'm pretty sure that's in bannock!"

Awâsis gratefully took Wâpos's offering. She rubbed
Wâpos's belly and continued on her way.

At the stream, Awâsis saw Ayîkis jumping from stone to stone. **"TÂN'SI NITÔTEM,"** Awâsis yelled, **"DO YOU KNOW WHERE I CAN FIND SOME BANNOCK?"**

Ayîkis stopped her leaps and croaked, "Namoya, Awâsis, but I have some sîwinikan, and I'm pretty sure that's in bannock!"

Awâsis gratefully accepted Ayîkis's offering. Awâsis jumped over the tiny stream and continued on her way.

Awâsis walked into the forest. In the branches of
a tall tree, she spotted Ôhô drifting off to sleep.
"Tân'si nitôtem," Awâsis whispered. "Do you know
where I can find some bannock?"

Ôhô awoke and looked down at Awâsis.
They swiveled their head back and forth and hooted,
"Namoya, Awâsis, but I have some sîwihtâkan,
and I'm pretty sure that's in bannock!"

Awâsis gratefully received Ôhô's offering but frowned a bit. "What's wrong?" Ôhô asked. Awâsis replied, "I have all these ingredients, but no bannock! Nôhkom is going to be so disappointed."

Ôhô hooted and laughed, "But Awâsis, your Kôhkum's recipe is so famous even I've heard of it. Truth be told, I can hear very well. You have most of the ingredients now, but check with your Kôhkum first!" And Ôhô flew away.

Awâsis raced straight home – no jumping on rocks or skipping over bridges. She stumbled through the door. "I'm sorry, Kôhkum! I dropped your world-famous bannock off a bridge. I asked many animal friends for help to find some more, but they gave me all these ingredients instead."

Kôhkum laughed. "It's okay, nôsisim,
we can make some more. Together!"

"But we still need some tohtôsâpoy."

Just then, Kôhkum and Awâsis heard a knock at the door. It was Maskwa with some tohtôsâpoy, offering it to both of them.

Kôhkum laughed some more. Then she and Awâsis began to make world-famous bannock to share with Awâsis's new friends.

Kôhkum's World-Famous Bannock

Ingredients

1 cup tohtosapopimehkan (margarine)

5–6 cups askipahkwesikan (flour)

3 tablespoons opihkasikan (baking powder)

2 tablespoons sîwinikan (sugar)

½ teaspoon sîwihtâkan (salt)

3 cups tohtôsâpoy (milk)

How to Bake

1. Preheat oven to 400°F (205°C).

2. In a large mixing bowl, combine all ingredients. Mix with hands. Add more flour if dough is too sticky.

3. Roll or spread out dough on a flour-dusted counter. Make sure dough is approximately half an inch thick.

4. Make biscuit shapes with a cup.

5. Poke top of bannock with the back of a spoon.

6. Bake for 20 minutes or until top begins to brown.

7. Now you have some pahkwesikan (bannock). *Be sure to share it with your friends!*

Cree	English	Pronunciation
awâsis	child	a-wah-sis
kôhkum*	grandmother	cook-um
sîsîp	duck	see-seep
tân'si	hello (how are you?)	tan-see
nitôtem	my friend	ni-toe-tem
nôhkom	my grandmother	nook-um
tohtosapopimehkan	margarine	toe-toe-sapo-pimay-gan
wâpos	rabbit	wah-pus
namoya	no	na-moy-a
askipahkwesikan	flour	aski-pahk-way-skun
ayîkis	frog	a-yee-kiss
sîwinikan	sugar	see-win-gan
ôhô	owl	oo-hoo
sîwihtâkan	salt	see-wee-tah-gan
nôsisim	grandchild	no-sim
tohtôsâpoy	milk	toe-toe-sa-poy
maskwa	bear	mask-wah
pahkwesikan	bannock	pahk-way-skun

*Note: These are Cree words as I have come to know them, through speaking with family members, elders, teachers, and fellow language-learners, as well as through reading books and dictionaries on nêhiyawêwin (the Cree language). One of the characters, Kôhkum, is a variation of the word kôhkom, which when translated means "your grandmother." However, kôhkum and other variations like kookum are widely used colloquially among many Indigenous communities to refer to their grandmother(s), so I've used the informal way of saying grandmother throughout, except when I mean "my grandmother," in which case I've used "nôhkom." Most importantly, this book is about having fun with Cree language revitalization, so all Cree speakers and learners should feel comfortable with this book and with their language, using whatever version of kôhkum feels best or makes sense to them! hiy hiy!   — D.H.

Canada Council **Conseil des Arts**
for the Arts **du Canada**

We acknowledge the support of the Canada Council for the Arts.
Nous remercions le Conseil des arts du Canada de son soutien.

HighWater Press gratefully acknowledges the financial support of the Province of Manitoba through the Department of Sport, Culture and Heritage and the Manitoba Book Publishing Tax Credit, and the Government of Canada through the Canada Book Fund (CBF), for our publishing activities.

HighWater Press is an imprint of Portage & Main Press.
Printed and bound in Canada by Friesens
Design by Relish New Brand Experience
Additional Illustrators: Dora Cepic, Natty Boonmasiri, Alex Mesa, Rasheed Banda

Library and Archives Canada Cataloguing in Publication

Issued in print and electronic formats.
Includes some text in Cree.
ISBN 978-1-55379-779-1 (hardcover)--ISBN 978-1-55379-781-4 (EPUB).--
ISBN 978-1-55379-780-7 (PDF)

    I. Strong, Amanda, 1984-, illustrator II. Title.

PS8615.U676A94 2018   jC813'.6   C2018-905257-0
                                         C2018-905258-9

22 21 20 19   2 3 4 5 6

HIGHWATER
PRESS
www.highwaterpress.com
Winnipeg, Manitoba
Treaty 1 Territory and homeland of the Métis Nation